Highest Total:

903 for 7 wickets by England against Australia
at the Oval, 1938.

Lowest Total:

45 by England against Australia at Sydney, 1886-7.

Highest Individual Score:

L. Hutton 364, at the Oval, 1938.

Highest Number of Wickets in a Match:

19 taken by J. C. Laker, at Manchester, 1956.

Batsmen Scoring Two Centuries in a Test Match:

H. Sutcliffe 176 and 127 at Melbourne, 1924-25.

W. R. Hammond 119 not out and 177
at Adelaide, 1928-29.

D. C. S. Compton 147 and 103 not out
at Adelaide, 1946-47.

Series 606C

With superb colour illustrations and a fairly simple vocabulary, this book tells the story of Cricket from the days when it was first played in England (more than five hundred years ago) up to the present day Test Matches.

It will encourage many young readers to get extra reading practice.

A LADYBIRD 'EASY-READING' BOOK

THE STORY OF CRICKET

by
VERA SOUTHGATE, M.A., B.Com.

with illustrations by
JACK MATTHEW

Publishers: Wills & Hepworth Ltd., Loughborough
First published 1964   ©   *Printed in England*

THE STORY OF CRICKET

The game of cricket was played in England more than five hundred years ago. Although, at that time, it was not the same as the game we now call cricket.

There were two different games, each a little like cricket. They were called club ball and stool ball.

In the game of club ball, there was a batsman, a bowler and fielders. The ball was covered with leather. The batsman used a stick or pole to hit the ball, but there was no wicket for him to defend.

7214 0075 2

In the game of stool ball, a stool was used as a wicket. The bowler tried to hit the stool with the ball and one man tried to stop him.

The man who was defending the stool did not have a bat. He just hit the ball with his bare hand.

The batsman did not score 'runs' as cricketers do nowadays. But, every time he defended his stool against a ball, he scored one point.

The batsman was 'out' if the ball hit the stool, or if the ball was caught by a fieldsman after the batsman had hit it.

Many years later, the batsman used a stick, instead of his hand, to defend the stool.

Then sticks began to be used for wickets. There were two wickets about twenty-two yards apart. Each one was made of three sticks. Two sticks were stuck upright in the ground with a third stick across the top. The sticks were often just branches of trees.

Sometimes, when shepherds wanted to play cricket, they could not find branches. Then they took a wicket gate from one of their sheep pens and used it as a wicket.

As more cricket was played, the batsman's stick was made into a bat. Then he began to score 'runs'; by running between the two wickets.

A hole was cut in the ground, between the two upright sticks of the wicket. The batsman had to put his bat in this hole, at the end of every run.

The batsman was 'run out' if the wicket keeper put the ball into this popping hole, before the batsman got his bat into it. Many wicket keepers had their fingers hurt in this way.

The two upright sticks of the wicket were so far apart that the ball could pass between them. So a third stick was put in the middle of the wicket.

Then there was no space for a popping hole, so a new rule was made. The umpire held up a stick. The batsman had to touch this stick, with his bat, at the end of every run.

There were just as many hurt fingers, with this rule, as when the popping hole was used. Then, at last, a 'popping crease' was marked on the grass, in front of the wicket, as it is in cricket to-day.

As cricket became a popular game in England, many cricket clubs were formed. Hambledon Cricket Club, which started in the year 1750, became the most famous of all.

At the Hambledon Club, the rules of cricket were written down and clubs all over the country agreed to them. Different ways of bowling, fielding and wicket-keeping were tried out.

At this time, for every run that a batsman made, a notch was cut in a stick. The runs were called the 'score', because the word 'score' means a scratch or mark. The man who cut out the notches was called the 'scorer'.

When cricket was first played, the bowler always sent the ball to the batsman with an under-arm throw.

About one hundred and fifty years ago, a young lady was trying to bowl for her brother. She wore a crinoline dress with a long, full skirt. The skirt had hoops in it to make it stand out stiffly.

When she tried to bowl under-arm, her crinoline stopped her arm swinging forward. She then began to swing her arm backwards and upwards, to throw the ball from above her head. Now all cricketers bowl over-arm instead of under-arm.

In under-arm bowling the ball travelled along the ground. Then the bat was made wider at the bottom than at the top.

Over-arm bowling made the ball bounce in front of the batsman. Then a straight bat began to be used. The early rules did not say how wide the bat should be.

At one match at Hambledon, a batsman used a bat almost twelve inches wide. It was as wide as the wicket. No one was able to bowl him out. The rule was then made that a bat could not be wider than four-and-a-half inches.

At first, cricket was played mostly by country people. Later, gentlemen in London began to play and many cricket clubs were formed there.

The most famous London club was near Marylebone Road. It was started by a man called Thomas Lord and it was called Marylebone Cricket Club. Now it is so well known that people hardly ever use its proper name. It is just spoken of as M.C.C.

The M.C.C. cricket ground was always called 'Lords', after Thomas Lord. Twice the club moved to new grounds. Each time, Thomas Lord arranged for the turf to be dug up and moved to the new ground.

In the early days of cricket, the players did not wear special clothes for the game. They just took off their jackets. Men who wore top hats, kept them on while they were playing.

Sometimes a player used his top hat to catch the ball. Some people thought that a ball caught in a top hat was not a fair catch.

Finally, a rule was made, saying that the ball should not be caught in a hat. If a player did this, five extra runs were given to the other team.

Now all men playing in cricket matches wear white clothes. Every player wears long white trousers, white boots, a white shirt and often a white sweater.

Cricketers wear special caps with wide peaks, which help to keep the sun out of their eyes.

Most cricket clubs have their own special club colours and club badges. The cricketer's cap, and the blazer which he wears when he is off the field, are in the club colours. The club badge is usually on the front of the cap and on the blazer pocket.

When the bowling in cricket became very fast, the players were more likely to be hurt by the ball. Then special pads and gloves were needed to protect them.

Nowadays the batsman wears heavy pads of leather and canvas, which are fastened onto his legs. His gloves are padded to protect his fingers.

The wicket keeper needs special protection. His pads are bigger and stronger than the batsman's. The wicket keeper wears very large leather gloves, with strong fingers and padded palms. Then, the fastest ball does not hurt his hands, as long as he catches it cleanly.

When cricket was first played, no one bothered about how many players should be on each side. Sometimes there were only a few players in a team, while at other times there were very large numbers.

When cricket rules were first made, there was no rule to say how many players should be on each side. Yet, for big matches, there were usually eleven men in each team.

In some of the South Sea islands, the game is very different. There, cricket matches are played between two villages. Every man in each village joins in the game, which may last for a week or more.

Now the rule is that a cricket team must always have eleven players. The side which goes in to bat first, usually sends its two best batsmen to open the innings.

The positions of the men in the fielding team are not always the same. Their positions are altered to suit the bowling. The captain of the fielding team, and the bowler, decide where to place the fieldsmen.

For a fast bowler, more fieldsmen are placed behind the batsman's wicket, than for a medium-pace bowler or a spin bowler. The picture shows how the field might be set for a medium-pace schoolboy bowler.

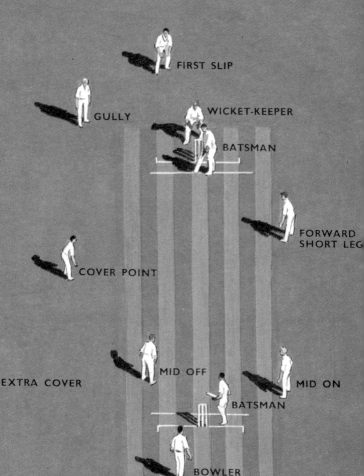

THIRD MAN

LONG LEG

FIRST SLIP

GULLY

WICKET-KEEPER

BATSMAN

FORWARD SHORT LEG

COVER POINT

EXTRA COVER

MID OFF

MID ON

BATSMAN

BOWLER

Cricketers must practise a lot, if they want to become good players. When they have plenty of time, and if twenty-two men are free, they sometimes have practice matches. But this is not the only way of practising cricket.

Most cricketers spend many hours practising 'at the nets'. This is a cricket wicket with netting on three sides of it. When the ball has been hit by a batsman, the netting stops it going very far. In this way, a few players can practise batting and bowling, without having to chase the ball a long way.

Cricket spread from England to other countries in the British Empire. Then Test Matches were played between these countries and England.

Australia first defeated England, in a Test Match, at the Oval, in 1882. Then it was said, as a joke, that English cricket was dead and that the Australian team would take the dead ashes back to Australia.

The next year, an English team defeated the Australian team, in Australia. In fun, the English team was presented with an urn of ashes to take back to England. Since then, in Test Matches between England and Australia, the winning team is always given "The Ashes".

Test Matches are now played between England, Australia, New Zealand, South Africa, India, Pakistan and the West Indies. Many people go to watch these Test Matches. The people who watch are called spectators.

Other games which spectators enjoy are the county matches. Many counties in England have cricket teams who play each other during the cricket season. Points are given to the winning team at each match. At the end of the season, the county team with the most points is called the County Champions.

Nowadays, many people who cannot go to Test Matches or County Matches, enjoy watching them on television.

The cricket grounds, on which Test Matches and County Matches are played, are looked after very carefully. Groundsmen cut the grass, water it and roll it. Special care is taken of the 'cricket square', in the centre of the field. This is where the stumps are set up.

Before a match, the umpires walk out on to the field to 'inspect the wicket'. They make sure that the ball will bounce and that the bowlers will be able to keep their feet. If there has been a lot of rain and the ground is too soft, the umpires may declare the ground to be 'unfit for play'.

The spectators, at a big cricket match, enjoy watching, as much as the teams enjoy playing.

At the large cricket grounds, each row of seats is built higher than the row in front. In this way, every one can have a good view of the match.

On a fine summer day many people spend hours watching cricket matches. The women and girls wear pretty summer dresses, and the men and boys take off their jackets. The spectators often eat ice-cream or drink orangeade, as they watch. There are also large tents in the cricket ground, where people can have lunch or tea.

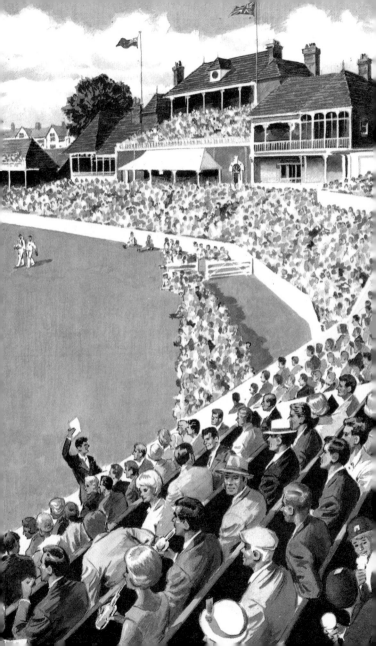

Nearly every large cricket ground now has a very big scoreboard. This board tells the spectators about the game, so that they know exactly what is happening.

Every player on the field has a number on the board. The batsmen's scores, and the total scores of the teams, are shown on the board. The scores are altered every time a run is made.

Some of the newest scoreboards even show which of the fieldsmen has the ball. A light flashes on the board, beside the fieldsman's number, as he handles the ball.

The umpires decide when a player is out and how many runs have been scored. They give special signals to show the scorer and the spectators what they have decided.

To show that a batsman is out, the umpire lifts the first finger of his right hand, in front of his head.

If a batsman hits a ball which rolls over the boundary, the umpire waves his right arm below shoulder level. This means that the batsman scores four runs. If the ball crosses the boundary, without touching the ground, the batsman scores six runs. The umpire signals this by lifting his arms above his head.

Nowadays, there are women's cricket teams, as well as men's teams. The women have county teams and play matches for County Championships.

Teams of women come from Australia and New Zealand to play matches against a team of English women. These teams are called touring teams and they play on the important cricket grounds, such as Lord's and the Oval. An English women's touring team also visits Australia and New Zealand.

For their matches, women cricketers wear white clothes, as men do. The women wear white blouses and shorts, and white shoes and stockings.

Cricket is not only a game for men and women. It is a game that is enjoyed by both boys and girls, although boys play it more often than girls do.

Many children now learn to play cricket at school. Games teachers give special coaching lessons, in which children learn to bat, bowl and field properly.

Cricket matches between school teams are played and school championships are arranged. In school matches, the boys wear white trousers and shirts, just as men's teams do. The boys have school blazers and caps, instead of club colours.

Although cricket is a game that is meant to be played on a field, boys play it in many different places.

In a street, or in a yard, boys who want to play cricket, often chalk wickets on walls or doors.

Cricket is often played at the seaside. The smooth, flat beach, after the tide has gone out, makes a good cricket pitch. Boys and girls like to set up stumps here and begin a game of cricket. Fathers often roll up their trouser legs and join in the game. It adds to the fun when the batsman manages to hit a 'boundary' into the sea.

Series 606C